ALIS

185125

D1419456

OXFORD BOOKWORMS LIBRARY
Fantasy & Horror

Voodoo Island

Stage 2 (700 headwords)

Series Editor: Jennifer Bassett
Founder Editor: Tricia Hedge
Activities Editors: Jennifer Bassett and Alison Baxter

MICHAEL DUCKWORTH

Voodoo Island

OXFORD UNIVERSITY PRESS

OXFORD
UNIVERSITY PRESS

Great Clarendon Street, Oxford OX2 6DP

Oxford University Press is a department of the University of Oxford.
It furthers the University's objective of excellence in research, scholarship,
and education by publishing worldwide in

Oxford New York

Auckland Cape Town Dar es Salaam Hong Kong Karachi
Kuala Lumpur Madrid Melbourne Mexico City Nairobi
New Delhi Shanghai Taipei Toronto

With offices in

Argentina Austria Brazil Chile Czech Republic France Greece
Guatemala Hungary Italy Japan Poland Portugal Singapore
South Korea Switzerland Thailand Turkey Ukraine Vietnam

OXFORD and OXFORD ENGLISH are registered trade marks of
Oxford University Press in the UK and in certain other countries

ISBN 978 0 19 479075 8

A complete recording of this Bookworms edition of
Voodoo Island is available on audio CD ISBN 978 0 19 478998 1

Printed in Hong Kong

Illustrated by: Caroline della Porta
Illustration on p 49 by: Neil Gower

CONTENTS

STORY INTRODUCTION   i

1   Island in the Sun   1
2   The Book of Baron Samedi   7
3   The Building Business   10
4   The Voodoo Man   13
5   The Graveyard   16
6   Conway has a Visitor   22
7   Conway's Hopes   23
8   The Spirit of the Wind and the Rain   27
9   Voodoo Law   35

GLOSSARY   40
ACTIVITIES: Before Reading   44
ACTIVITIES: While Reading   45
ACTIVITIES: After Reading   48
ABOUT THE AUTHOR   52
ABOUT THE BOOKWORMS LIBRARY   53

1

Island in the Sun

James Conway put away his business papers and sat back in his seat. He looked out of the aeroplane window down at the warm blue sea below. Far away, in the bright sun, there were the long white beaches of the island of Haiti. Behind them, he could just see the small wooden houses and the deep green leaves of the coconut trees, which were moving lazily in the soft afternoon wind.

'It looks beautiful, doesn't it?' Conway looked at the

The coconut trees were moving slowly in the wind.

woman sitting next to him. 'Very nice,' he answered.

'Is this your first visit to Haiti?' the woman asked.

'Yes, but I'm not here as a visitor,' said Conway. 'I have a building company – it's called Conway Construction. My company has offices all over the world – America, Europe, Africa. We're very big in Australia too – everyone in Australia has heard the name Conway. I'm coming to get an office here, buy some land, build a few hotels, you know. The land is very cheap here – you can buy a piece of land to build a small town on, for a few thousand dollars. Sorry, I don't know your name. I'm Mr Conway, James Conway. Just call me Conway.'

'I'm Karen Jackson.'

'Nice to meet you, Karen. What do you do? Have you got a job, or are you married?'

'I'm at Harvard University.'

'From the University? Are you a secretary there?'

'No, I'm a doctor. I'm teaching medicine.'

'A doctor! That's interesting. What are you doing here in Haiti? Are you on holiday? I know you teachers get long holidays.'

Karen Jackson was beginning to dislike the man.

'No,' she said. 'I'm going to work in the hospital at Port au Prince. And while I'm here, I'm going to do some work for my book.'

'Voodoo works, and it can be very dangerous.'

'Are you writing a book? What is it about?'

'Voodoo.'

'Voodoo!' laughed Conway. 'Are you telling me that someone is paying you to come here and write about voodoo? I know Haiti is not America, but voodoo! I thought people stopped believing in that years ago.'

'Oh, no,' said Karen. 'People still believe in it. You see, it works, and it can be very dangerous.'

'Surely you don't believe in voodoo, do you?'

'Yes, I do. We don't really understand voodoo in

'The doll's face is a coconut, and there's a pin in its stomach.'

4

America. Most people think it's magic. They think it can kill people.'

'That's right. I remember hearing about it. People who use voodoo get a picture of a person or make a doll, don't they? Then they put pins or knives into it, and the person feels terrible pain.'

'Yes, that's right,' Karen answered. 'I have a photograph here in one of my books about voodoo. Look, there's one of the dolls. It's not a child's doll – it's made from coconuts. You see, the face is a coconut, and someone has drawn eyes, a nose, and a mouth on it. And look, there's a pin in the doll's stomach. A few days later the man came to hospital because his stomach hurt. He knew that someone was using voodoo against him. The pain was terrible, but the doctors couldn't find anything wrong with him. In the end, he died.'

Conway was surprised. 'So you think that was magic because there was no reason for it,' he said. 'But you're a doctor, aren't you? You don't believe in magic, do you?'

'Voodoo is more than magic. I don't believe in magic, but I know that voodoo can be very dangerous. I want to understand how it works. Here in Haiti there are still a few people who know how to use voodoo. They are called "houngans". There are still a few "houngans" in the villages in the country. And that's why I'm here. I want to meet some of them and talk to them. Of course they aren't all bad people. They can use voodoo to help people, like doctors. But they can use it to hurt people too.'

'But we're living in the modern world!'

'Yes, but the people here are very sure that voodoo is real. Teachers, business people, doctors, everyone believes in it . . . or they are afraid of it. And perhaps that's why it works. After all, if you believe you are ill, you can be ill. And if you really think you're getting better, you can get better. If you think that someone is trying to kill you, then you can die . . . because you are so afraid.'

'Well, that's a good story,' laughed Conway. 'If I need some voodoo, I'll come and see you.'

'OK,' said Karen. 'Excuse me for a minute.' She got up and walked to the back of the plane. She was bored and angry with Conway, because he thought he understood everything and he never listened to other people.

The Book of Baron Samedi

While she was away, Conway looked at the open book on her seat. There was a picture on the page which showed a black man with open eyes and bright white teeth. He was laughing, but he looked frightening and dangerous. Conway read the words below the picture:

'Baron Samedi, the strongest and most dangerous of all the voodoo houngans. No one knows who Baron Samedi is, but they believe he is both dead and alive. He lives in two different worlds. Many people are so frightened of him that they are afraid to say his name.'

Baron Samedi, the strongest of the voodoo houngans.

Conway looked at the picture. 'Baron Samedi!' he laughed. 'How can these people be so stupid? Still, it will be easy to make money if they think like children.'

A few minutes later, Karen came back. She picked up the book and put it in her bag. As she was sitting down, the lights in the aeroplane came on.

'We are going to arrive at Port au Prince airport in a few minutes. Please stay in your seats and put out your cigarettes. The time in Haiti is 3.15. It is a warm day and it is 30°C. We hope you have enjoyed flying with Air Haiti, and we hope that you will fly with us again. Thank you.'

Down below them, in the village of Bussy, not far from Port au Prince, Kee was in his small wooden house among the trees. Outside, a few brown chickens were trying to find something to eat in the garden. There was not much rain in the summer and the ground was dry and dusty. The old man Kee was sitting by the window in the front room. Suddenly he felt that something was wrong. In the garden the wind blew harder, and the dust from the dry ground flew into the air. He stood up, went to the window and looked out.

'I can feel danger,' he thought. 'Someone bad is coming.' He looked out into the trees, but he couldn't

Kee was in his small wooden house among the trees.

see anything. Then he looked up at the sky, and saw the plane just before it went behind a cloud on its way to Port au Prince airport.

3

The Building Business

After nine months in Haiti, Conway was a happy man. His business was going well, and he was making a lot of money. He had a large office in Port au Prince, a big house, and hundreds of people were working for him. He had some land near Port au Prince, and he was building a new town. There were already hundreds of new houses, and many people knew the name Conway Construction. But Conway had a problem, and he wanted to see a business friend, Jacques Remy.

The telephone on his desk rang. He picked it up. 'Yes?'

'Mr Remy is here to see you, Mr Conway,' said his secretary.

'Send him in immediately.' A few moments later, Jacques Remy came into the room.

'Jacques, it's nice to see you. Thank you for coming. Sit down.'

'Thanks,' said Jacques. 'You said on the phone that you had a problem.'

'Yes,' said Conway. 'You helped me buy the land for the new town when I first came to Haiti. Some of the houses are ready, and people are living in them. But now I need more land.'

'You can buy land anywhere,' said Jacques.

'I know, but I want a piece of land near my houses. People will need shops, and perhaps I can build a hotel too, and some more houses.'

'What piece of land do you want?' asked Jacques.

'Well, that's the problem.' Conway took out a pencil

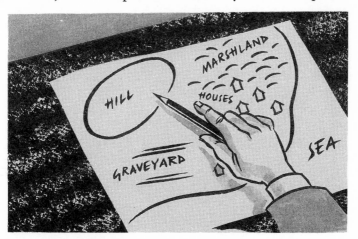

'I can only build the shops and houses on this hill.'

11

and a piece of paper, and began to draw a map. 'Most of the houses are here,' he said. 'Now, I can't build on the south or the east side of the houses because of the sea. On the north side the land is no good. There is too much water in it. So I can only build on the west side. I can only build on this hill.'

'Good,' said Jacques. 'Buy the hill and then you can build more houses on the other side too.'

'I want to,' said Conway, 'but there's a problem.' He went over to the desk and picked up a photograph. It was a photograph of a graveyard. He gave the photograph of the graveyard to Jacques. 'You see, it won't be easy. I want to build on the graveyard.'

Jacques looked at the photograph carefully. 'It's very

'I want to build on this graveyard.'

old,' he said, 'and that's good. If only a few people go there, perhaps you can buy it. But if it is new and a lot of people go there, they will be angry, and it will be difficult to buy it. Go and look at the stones. Find out how old the place is. I'll talk to some friends. Perhaps they can help.'

'Thank you very much, Jacques. I won't forget this.'

'It's nothing,' said Jacques. 'Tell me how old the stones are, and I'll ring you again in a few days.'

4

The Voodoo Man

A big lorry drove past Kee's house. It was going very fast and it made a lot of noise. Before Conway built the new town, Kee's village was a quiet place. There were only a few small cars. Now big lorries went past every five minutes, carrying things for the new buildings. Kee was a very unhappy old man. He was sitting in his small house, looking out into the garden.

Another big lorry went past the window.

He heard the sound of a car coming down the road. The car stopped near the house, and a woman got out.

13

She was young and well dressed. She walked up to the gate at the end of Kee's garden and waited. Kee saw her and went out of the house, down the wooden steps and into the garden.

'Hello,' she said, looking at the old man. 'Can I come in?'

'Yes, of course,' answered Kee. 'What can I do for you?'

The woman opened the gate and came up to Kee. 'My name is Karen Jackson,' she said, 'Dr Jackson. I'm an American. I'm working at the big hospital in Port au Prince, and I'm doing some work for my book.'

'I see,' said Kee. 'But why do you want to talk to me?'

Karen Jackson walked up to the gate of Kee's garden.

'I'm writing a book about voodoo,' she said. 'Everyone here talks about you. They all say you are the best houngan in Haiti. They say you are a very strong and good houngan, and that you always help people.'

Kee smiled. 'I try to help good people,' he said. 'Come into the house, Dr Jackson. Let me get you a drink and we can talk.'

Kee and Karen went into the house and began to talk. Karen told him about her life and her work, and why she was in Haiti. Kee told her about his life and talked for a long time about the old Haiti and the people he remembered.

'Everything is changing,' he said. 'When I was a young man, we lived with our families. We worked in the coffee fields. We helped each other. Friends were more important than money. People were good and kind. But everything is different now. Business people come from America and Europe and start banks and big companies. All the young men go to Port au Prince. They leave their villages and their families. They think about money all the time. They don't think about people.'

'Yes, I know,' said Karen. 'It's happening in America too. But you can always find good people if you look for them.'

'I know,' said Kee, smiling. 'You don't have to go back yet, do you?'

'No, not yet. Why?'

'There's something that I want to show you. It's a hill outside the village. I often go there when I'm unhappy, or when I want to think. It's a graveyard, but it's very beautiful there, when the warm wind blows the leaves of the coconut trees.'

5

The Graveyard

They left his house and began to walk along the road to the hill. When they arrived, they walked slowly through the graveyard. At the top of the hill, they looked down at the fields below. They could see a lot of lorries, and a lot of men were working there, building the new town. Already there were hundreds and hundreds of new houses in the field. 'The village is changing very fast,' he said. 'Soon there are going to be thousands and thousands of new houses. What will happen to our village then? Once it was a quiet place and the people were friendly. But soon there will be a lot of new people and busy, noisy roads. I don't want to live in a place like that.'

'Can't you do anything? Can't you stop them?' asked Karen.

'Me? No. What can I do? Nothing. I'm an old man, and nobody listens to me.'

They walked on through the graveyard, and Kee said, 'My grandfather is here in this graveyard. He was my mother's father. I remember the day when he died. I cried for a long time when I saw that big dark hole in the ground, and we put his body in the grave. It was raining. I was twelve years old. My mother and father were with me, and they were crying too.'

Karen and Kee walked through the graveyard.

'I'm sorry,' said Karen.

'Oh, it was a long time ago,' said Kee. 'But my grandfather's grave was the last on this hill. After he died, they made a new graveyard on the other side of the village. That's why nobody comes here now. Nobody remembers the old people here.'

'But you do.'

'Oh, yes. I could never forget my grandfather. He taught me about voodoo, about the spirit of the rain and the spirit of the wind. You see, nothing is really dead. There's a spirit in everything, in every tree, in the sun, in the sea. If you understand voodoo, you can talk to these spirits. And there's a spirit under this cold grey stone.'

Kee showed her the stone on his grandfather's grave and Karen read the words slowly. 'Tim Atty. Born 1845. Died 1906.' Kee looked at Karen and said quietly, 'Some people say he was the strongest houngan of all, the houngan we call Baron Samedi.'

'Baron Samedi!' cried Karen. 'Your grandfather!' Suddenly she felt afraid when she heard the terrible name. She looked at the old man.

'I see you know more about voodoo than I thought,' he said. 'But don't be afraid of me. I'm just an old man who doesn't like the new world.' He smiled at Karen again.

'Some people say he was the houngan, *Baron Samedi.'*

They stayed on the hill and talked for a long time. Then Karen looked at her watch and said, 'What? Is that the time? I'm sorry, Kee, but I must go now. I have to be at the hospital at four o'clock.' Kee got up.

'Don't worry,' said Karen. 'I can find the car – it's not far. Please stay if you want to.'

'Are you sure?'

'Yes, I know how to get back.'

'Well, then, I think I'll stay a little longer. It was very nice to talk to you.'

'Thank you for talking to me, too. I've learnt a lot today. I hope we'll meet again.'

'I hope so too. Goodbye.'

19

Kee watched Karen as she walked down the hill. And then he saw two men. They were young, and they were carrying lots of papers. They walked around the graveyard for a short time, looking at the graves and then at the papers. Kee went over to them.

'Good afternoon,' he said.

'Good afternoon,' the men replied.

'What are you doing here?' asked Kee.

'We work for Conway Construction,' they said. 'We're building some shops here.'

'And a big hotel,' said the other man. Kee was very

'My grandfather's grave is here.'

20

surprised. 'What?' he said. 'You can't do that here. This is a graveyard. You can't build houses and shops in a graveyard. It's a very important place.'

The two men laughed at him. 'Don't be stupid, old man,' they said. 'This graveyard is very old. Nobody comes here now. The people in this graveyard died a hundred years ago.'

Kee was angry. 'Don't talk to me like that,' he said. 'My grandfather's grave is here. You're not going to build shops and houses on this land.'

One of the men said, 'Yes, we are. This is Mr Conway's land. He bought it a few days ago. He's going to build shops here and we're going to help him.'

'No,' said Kee. 'That isn't true.'

'It is true,' replied the man. 'We're going to start next week. If you want to, you can go and see Mr Conway. You can talk to him. He'll tell you it's true.'

'Where does he live?' asked Kee. The men gave him a small piece of paper. He looked at it. The paper said: 'Conway Construction, 16 Rue de la République, Port au Prince.'

Kee said, 'Don't begin any work here. I want to see Conway first. I'll tell him that he can't build shops here.'

The two men laughed and said, 'OK, old man. We'll wait for you.'

6

Conway has a Visitor

The next morning Kee got on the bus. He bought a ticket to Port au Prince. During the journey he looked out of the window. There were new houses and offices all along the road from his village to Port au Prince.

When he arrived, he found a taxi and gave the driver the address. 'Do you know how to get there?' asked Kee.

'Oh, yes,' said the taxi driver. 'Mr Conway is a big man round here. Very important. Rich, too. And they say he has a lot of friends.'

'I know,' said Kee. He sat back in the taxi as it drove away.

After a long time, they arrived at the office of Conway Construction. Kee paid the taxi driver, and went in. Conway's secretary, Marie, was sitting at a desk. She looked at Kee.

'Good afternoon,' she said, 'Can I help you?'

'Yes,' said Kee, 'I want to talk to Mr Conway.'

'What's your name?' the young woman asked.

'Kee,' he replied.

'Please sit down,' Marie said. Then she picked up a

telephone and talked to Conway. 'There's a man here,' she said. 'He wants to talk to you.' She waited for a moment, and then said, 'Kee, Mr Kee. No, I don't know who he is. He's an old man.' Marie put down the telephone and looked at Kee. 'Mr Conway is waiting for you,' she said. 'Please go in.'

Kee walked to Conway's door and went in. Conway smiled and said, 'Good afternoon, Kee. My name is Conway. Please sit down. Can I help you?' Kee was surprised. Then he said, 'Yes, Mr Conway. My name is Kee. I live in the village of Bussy.'

'Do you?' said Conway. 'I know the village of Bussy well. It's very nice. We're building a new town there.'

'Yes, I know,' said Kee. 'You're building some shops and a hotel there too. But you must not build them on the graveyard. It is a very important place.'

7

Conway's Hopes

Kee looked at Conway. He said, 'I am a houngan, and I understand voodoo. I know you come from America, and you Americans do not believe in things like that.

23

But I can do many things that you do not understand. I will help you if you are good to me.'

'You're very kind,' said Conway, laughing at the old man. 'But I really don't think your voodoo can give me all the things I want in life.'

'What do you want?'

'I want a lot of things,' said Conway.

'Tell me.'

'I want to live in a big house, with lots of rooms.'

'That will not be difficult,' said the old man.

'Oh, but I want more than that. I hate housework. I want lots of people to clean the rooms and bring me food. I want to have a lot of money in the bank. Oh,

'I want to live in a big house, with lots of rooms . . .'

24

and I don't want to work. I want a lot of things, you see.'

'All right,' said Kee. 'You can have those things.'

'That's very kind of you,' said Conway, laughing. 'Now, I've got work to do.'

But Kee sat quietly on his chair and smiled. 'I can see that you do not believe me,' he said. 'You think I'm just an old man who doesn't want to see new shops and houses. Just wait for a few days, and you will see. I'll give you everything that you want. But you must not build shops and hotels in the graveyard. Do you understand?'

'Yes, yes, yes, of course I understand,' said Conway. He was beginning to get angry. 'I won't build shops and hotels there, and you will give me everything I want. Thank you very much for your help. Now, please, get out. I'm a busy man.'

'Goodbye,' said Kee. 'Thank you for talking to me. But don't forget, Mr Conway, you must not do these things. If you do, you'll be sorry.'

'Yes, yes, yes, I understand. Now go!' said Conway.

Kee turned and went to the door. For a moment, as the old man was walking out of the door, Conway remembered the face in the book on the plane. Suddenly he felt cold and afraid.

When Kee left the room, Conway picked up the

telephone. He talked to Marie. He was very, very angry.

'Marie!' he shouted. 'Why did you send that man to my office? He's mad. Coming in here talking about voodoo! Telling me he's going to give me a lot of money! I don't want to see him again. Do you understand? If you make a mistake like that again, you'll lose your job.'

'I'm very sorry,' said Marie.

'Good. Now, I want to talk to Pierre and Henri. Get them on the telephone for me.' He put down the telephone and sat back in his chair. 'That man Kee is

'I don't want to see that mad man again.'

mad,' he thought. Then he started to laugh. 'He thinks he can give me everything I want!' he thought. 'An old man from a village! Ha, ha, ha!'

The telephone rang again. Conway picked it up. 'Pierre, Henri, listen,' he said. 'A few minutes ago an old man came to my office. He doesn't want any shops or houses in the graveyard. It's possible he'll try to stop us. I don't know what he can do, but perhaps he'll go to the police. Perhaps he has important friends. So you must start building the shops and the hotel today. Take away all the stones. Cut down all the trees. You must work fast, do you understand?'

Conway put down the telephone and thought, 'The old man will be angry, but he isn't important. I'll finish building my town and then I'll be a rich man.'

8

The Spirit of the Wind and the Rain

For many weeks Kee did not go back to the graveyard. He thought, 'I'm happy that I went to see Conway. He's a good man. He's not going to build shops and houses in the graveyard. The people in the graveyard are dead, but their spirits are not dead. The spirits will help him. The spirits will give him everything he wants. The spirit of the wind will bring him good luck and the spirit of the rain will make him happy.'

But one afternoon Kee went back to the graveyard again. There were no trees. There were no stones. There were no graves. But there were a lot of men in the graveyard. They were from Conway Construction and they were building the shops and the hotel. When Kee saw what was happening, he became terribly angry. His face went white and his hands began to shake. Kee ran up to the men and said, 'What's happening? Why are you building here in the graveyard?'

The men laughed at him and said, 'Go away, old man. This isn't a graveyard any more. We're building shops for the new town. Go back to your village and be quiet.'

Night came, and the village was very quiet. Kee was alone outside his house. In the garden there was a small fire and the yellow and orange flames danced in the dark, throwing strange black shapes across the ground. Kee took a stick and drew a circle in the ground. He walked round and round the circle, singing a strange song. A long way away, he could hear the sound of some dogs howling at the night sky.

Kee began to talk very quietly. He said, 'Spirit of the

28

'Spirit of the wind, something bad must happen to Conway.'

wind, spirit of the rain, listen to me and help. His name is Conway. I saw him a few weeks ago. He said some things to me, but they were not true. Conway is building the shops and hotels in the graveyard. When I saw him I said, "I will give you everything you want." Now I need your help, because the things I say are always true. I do not want to give him everything he wants, but I must. That is the law of the houngan. But something bad must happen to him too. Spirit of the wind, spirit of the rain, help me, help me . . .'

When Kee finished, a cold wind began to blow. It blew through the village, and then the trees began to move in the wind. There were clouds in the sky, and it began to rain. Soon the wind and the rain came to Port au Prince.

Conway was getting ready to go to bed. Then the wind began to blow and he began to feel cold and afraid. He looked out of the window. It was very dark, and there were a lot of clouds in the sky. He picked up his clock and put it by his bed because he had to wake up at seven o'clock. Then he turned off the light. Just before he went to sleep, he could hear the wind and the rain in the garden, and he thought, for a moment, that he could see the face of an old man at the window.

He did not sleep well that night. All night he had bad

dreams, terrible dreams. In his dreams he saw Kee's grandfather and all the other spirits from the graveyard. He was very frightened of the spirits and they ran after him in his dreams. He saw their white faces and felt their cold hands. He could hear strange music coming from behind dark trees and could hear people screaming and laughing, and shouting out his name.

RRRRING! It was seven o'clock. Conway looked at his clock and got out of bed. He brushed his teeth. He was very tired after his bad night. But he washed his face with cold water, and he began to feel much better. He soon forgot about his dreams of Kee and the graveyard.

In his dream, Conway saw the spirits from the graveyard.

He got dressed, and then had some breakfast and opened his letters. At eight o'clock he got in his car and went to the office. Marie was not there, so he opened the doors and made a cup of coffee. He went into his office and sat down. He was sitting behind the big desk in his office when the telephone rang.

RRRRRING! Conway woke up. He was in bed. He looked around the room. 'What's happening?' he thought. 'Where am I?' He picked up his clock. It was seven o'clock. Conway thought, 'That was a dream again. In my dream I got up and went to the office. But it was only a dream, and I'm still at home. How strange! I thought I was at the office.'

Conway got dressed and went to the office. When he went in, Marie was sitting at her desk.

'Good morning, Marie,' he said.

'Good morning, Mr Conway,' she said. 'How are you?'

'I'm fine,' he said. 'But I had a strange dream last night. In my dream, I woke up and came to the office. Then I woke up and I was at home.'

'Well,' she said. 'You're here now. This time you're not dreaming.'

Conway went into his office and started to work. There was a knock on the door.

'Come in,' said Conway. An old man came into the

32

Was it the face from Karen Jackson's book?

office. He looked at Conway and started laughing.

'Hello, Conway,' said the old man. 'Do you know my name?' Conway looked at the old man and felt afraid. He knew the face. But where was it from? Whose face was it? Was it from the dream? . . . Or was it from a picture in a book? Was it the face from Karen Jackson's book?

'I am Kee's grandfather!' the old man said. And then he began to laugh and scream like a man who was mad.

33

Suddenly the telephone rang.

RRRRRRING! Conway woke up. He looked round the room. He was in bed. He looked at his clock – it was seven o'clock in the morning. He thought, 'I was dreaming again. But what's happening now? Am I sleeping or am I awake?' He was very frightened now. He got up and went to the bathroom to wash his face. He looked into the mirror and screamed. In front of him, in the mirror, there was the head of a dead man. There were no eyes, and no nose, just deep black holes. A long thin red snake was moving slowly in and out of the holes. The snake looked at him with its two small cold eyes, and moved through the open mouth and went round and round the neck, and stopped. Then suddenly the head came alive. It had bright white teeth, there were fires in the eyes, and it began to laugh and scream. Then Conway remembered the face. In front of him was the face of Kee's grandfather, the face of the terrible voodoo houngan, Baron Samedi, laughing at him.

RRRRRRRING! Conway woke up again. He was in bed. He looked at the clock. It was seven o'clock.

He started screaming.

Voodoo Law

A few weeks later Kee was in the garden outside his house. The village was quiet and there were no lorries or cars. It was early evening and Kee was giving the chickens some food as the sun went down. He heard a car coming along the road. He stopped and looked up. Karen Jackson stopped the car outside the gate and got out. Kee went over to meet her.

'Karen!' he said. 'Come in. It's very nice to see you again.'

'Thank you,' she said.

They went into the house, and Kee gave her a drink. They sat down and talked for a short time.

'Is something wrong?' asked Kee. 'You look worried, unhappy.'

'Yes. Yes, I am,' said Karen. 'That's why I'm here. I want to ask you something.'

'Yes, what is it?'

'Well, there's someone in the hospital who is very sick. We don't know what to do. Can you come to the hospital and help us?'

Kee laughed. 'American doctors don't usually ask

'There's someone in the hospital who is very sick.'

old men for help.'

Karen said, 'I know, but you're not an ordinary old man. You're different.'

'All right. I'll come. But I don't know if I can help.'

'You're very kind. When can you come?' asked Karen.

'Now, if you want. I'm not doing anything important.'

'Thank you,' said Karen. 'You're very kind. I've got a car. I can take you there.'

Karen and Kee drove out of the small village, down the road, and soon came to the houses of the new

36

town. They passed the hill, but she did not turn to look at the graveyard. There were a lot of lorries at the side of the road. Karen looked at the names on the side of the lorries – Conway Construction.

'They're building a lot more houses here too, aren't they?' said Karen.

'They *were*,' said Kee.

They did not talk any more on the way to the hospital. When they arrived, Karen drove into the doctors' car park and stopped the car. She got out and came round to open Kee's door. Then they walked up to the front door of the large hospital. The glass doors opened and they went in. As they walked through the hospital, Kee noticed the strange smell, the clean white walls, and the big glass doors. When they came to the desk, the nurse said 'hello' to Karen. She went round the desk to look in a book.

'Room 473,' she said, looking at Kee. 'It's this way.' They walked to the lift and went up to the fourth floor. The doors opened, and Karen took Kee to the room. There was a small window in the door of the room.

Karen stopped. 'Look!' she said. Kee looked through the small window into the room. There were no tables or chairs in the room, and there were no other windows. Next to the wall there was a bed.

Kee looked at the man in the bed. It was Conway. He was wearing a big white coat, and he was screaming. While Kee was looking at the man, Karen explained. 'His name is Conway, James Conway. It's strange. When I came to Haiti, we were on the same plane. He sat next to me. He wanted to start a business and make money. I didn't like him very much, I can tell you, but he wasn't mad. Look at him now. He's mad, and we don't know why. He doesn't talk to anyone and he starts screaming when he hears a telephone or a bell ringing. He's afraid of sleeping too, and we can't

'He has a big place to live in, with lots of rooms . . .'

do anything for him. Some of the nurses are saying he's like that because of voodoo.'

'Perhaps the nurses are right,' said Kee. Then he thought for a moment, and began to smile.

'Can you help him?' asked Karen.

'I'm sorry,' said Kee, 'I'm not a doctor. But perhaps he's happy here. He has a big place to live in, with lots of rooms. People come and clean the rooms and bring him food. He doesn't have to work, and he's got a lot of money in the bank. Perhaps he has everything he wants.'

Karen looked at the old man and for a moment she saw something cold and frightening in his smiling eyes.

GLOSSARY

awake not asleep

believe to think that something is true

bell when a telephone rings, the noise is made by a bell

blow (past tense **blew**) when air moves, a wind is blowing

clean *(v)* to work on something that is dirty and make it clean

coconut a large brown hard fruit that grows on trees in hot countries

company a group of people who work together to make money

construction building

doll a small model of a person; children play with dolls

draw (past tense **drew**) to make a picture with a pencil, pen, etc.

dream *(n)* pictures in your mind when you are asleep

dry not wet

dust *(n)* dry dirt that is like powder

dusty covered with dust

flame the yellow/orange part of a fire

frightened afraid

frightening if something is frightening, it makes you feel afraid

gate a kind of door in a wall or fence outside

grave a hole in the ground where the body of a dead person lies

graveyard a place with many graves

hope *(v)* to want something that you think will happen

houngan a person in Haiti who can use voodoo

howl *(v)* to make a long loud cry (like a dog makes)

land *(n)* ground used for building, etc.

law a law says that a person must, or must not, do something

lorry a kind of very large car that can carry big things

mad ill in the mind (the head)

magic when somebody makes strange things happen and nobody can understand or explain them

map a drawing of a town or country that shows roads, rivers, hills, etc.

medicine something that can make ill people well again

ordinary not strange or special

pain when something hurts, you feel pain

park (**car park**) a place where you can leave your car

pick up to take something in the hand

pin *(n)* a very small, sharp piece of metal

problem something difficult to understand, or find an answer for

snake a long thin animal without legs

spirit the part of a person that is not the body; some people think the spirit lives after the body dies

steps stairs outside a house, in a garden, a road, etc.

throw (past tense **threw**) to make something move through the air

university a place where people can study after they leave school

voodoo a special magic that is used in Haiti

Voodoo Island

ACTIVITIES

Before Reading

1 **Read the back cover and the story introduction on the first page of the book. What do you know now about voodoo? Use the words below to complete these sentences from the story.**

afraid, dangerous, hurt, spirit, voodoo

1 'Voodoo is more than magic. I don't believe in magic, but I know that voodoo can be very _____.'

2 'You see, nothing is really dead. There's a _____ in everything, in every tree, in the sun, in the sea. If you understand _____, you can talk to these spirits.'

3 'They can use voodoo to help people, like doctors. But they can use it to _____ people too.'

4 'Everyone believes in it . . . or they are _____ of it. And perhaps that's why it works.'

2 **Can you guess who will say these things – Kee or Conway?**

1 'I'll tell him that he can't build shops here.'

2 'Now, please, get out, I'm a busy man.'

3 'You must not do these things. If you do, you'll be sorry.'

4 'I'll finish building my town and then I'll be a rich man.'

While Reading

Read Chapters 1 and 2, and then answer these questions.

Who

1 . . . wanted to make a lot of money?
2 . . . was a young doctor who was interested in voodoo?
3 . . . lived in the worlds of both the dead and the living?
4 . . . felt danger was coming?

Read Chapter 3. Match these halves of sentences, and put them together using the words below.

so / but / because / and

1 After nine months in Haiti, Conway was happy _____
2 The first houses in the new town were finished, _____
3 He wanted to build on the hill to the west of the town,

  _____

4 He knew this was a problem, _____

5 now he needed some more land.
6 he called his business friend Jacques Remy.
7 he was making a lot of money.
8 there was an old graveyard on it.

Read Chapters 4 and 5. Are these sentences true (T) or false (F)? Change the false sentences into true ones.

1 Kee was happy about all the building work.
2 Karen came to ask Kee about the new houses.
3 Kee took Karen to see his grandfather's grave.
4 Karen did not know the name 'Baron Samedi'.
5 The men from Conway Construction laughed at Kee.

Read Chapters 6 and 7. Choose the best word to complete these sentences.

1 Kee went to see Conway because he was *sad / angry / afraid*.
2 Kee said, 'You mustn't build on the graveyard. It's a very *beautiful / old / important* place.'
3 When Kee left, Conway remembered the face in Karen's book, and he felt *frightened / happy / angry*.
4 Conway sent Kee away because he thought Kee was *stupid / mad / important*.

Complete this text with words from Chapter 7 (one word for each gap).

Conway wants to live in a _____ house with lots of _____.
He wants lots of people to _____ the rooms and bring him
_____. He wants to have a lot of _____ in the bank, and he
doesn't want to _____.

Before you read Chapters 8 and 9, can you guess the answers to these questions? The chapter titles are:

Chapter 8: The Spirit of the Wind and the Rain
Chapter 9: Voodoo Law

1 Will Conway build on the graveyard?
2 Will Conway learn any more about voodoo?
3 Will Kee give Conway all the things that he wants?
4 Will Kee use voodoo to do something bad to Conway?
5 Will Karen meet Conway again?

Read Chapter 8. Who said these things, and to whom?

1 'Go back to your village and be quiet.'
2 'Now I need your help.'
3 'This time you're not dreaming.'
4 'Do you know my name?'
5 'Am I sleeping or am I awake?'

Read Chapter 9, and then answer these questions.

1 What was Kee's village like now?
2 Why did Karen come to see Kee for a second time?
3 Who was in Room 473 in the hospital, and why?
4 What did he do when he heard a telephone or a bell?
5 What were the nurses saying about him?
6 Why did Kee say, 'But perhaps he's happy here'?

After Reading

1 **Choose the best words to complete this text about Kee.**

Kee is a *rich / poor* man who comes from *Haiti / America*.
He is a *businessman / houngan*, and he knows all about
money / spirits. He doesn't understand *voodoo / business*,
and / but he *understands / doesn't understand* about
people. Kee *is / is not* a kind man, and he *always / never*
listens to other people.

Now use the other words to write a text about Conway.

2 **What happened after Chapter 8? Put these sentences into
the right order, and rewrite them as a paragraph. Use
linking words (*and, but, so, then*) where possible.**

1 She called the police and an ambulance.

2 The ambulance took Conway to hospital.

3 She drove to Conway's house.

4 One day Conway did not arrive at work.

5 His secretary Marie rang him at home.

6 The policemen broke open the door.

7 Nobody answered the telephone.

8 She heard screaming from inside the house.

3 Here is a new illustration for the story. Find the best place in the book to put the picture, and answer these questions.

The picture goes on page ____.

1 Where is Kee?
2 Why is he angry?
3 Why are the men laughing at him?

Now write a caption for the illustration.

Caption: _____

4 **When Conway arrived at the hospital, Karen asked Marie some questions. Complete Marie's answers. (Use as many words as you like.)**

KAREN: Was Mr Conway unwell at work yesterday?

MARIE: No, doctor, he _____. But in the afternoon a strange old man _____ and _____.

KAREN: Why was Mr Conway angry? What happened?

MARIE: I don't really know. But when the old man left, Mr Conway shouted _____ and said _____.

KAREN: Mad? What did they talk about? Do you know?

MARIE: Mr Conway said that the old man was talking _____ and about giving _____.

KAREN: Voodoo! Why voodoo? What happened next?

MARIE: Mr Conway spoke to _____ and told them to start _____.

KAREN: The old graveyard? Was the old man's name Kee?

MARIE: Yes, it was. But why _____?

KAREN: Because he's a houngan. I think I understand now.

MARIE: Understand what? And what's _____?

KAREN: Mr Conway is sick because Kee has used voodoo against him. And I'm afraid we can't help him.

MARIE: Voodoo? You don't believe in all that, do you, doctor? No, I know what's wrong with him – he works too hard and drinks too much, that's all.

Imagine that you heard this conversation. Who do you agree with, Karen or Marie?

5 **What do you think happens after Chapter 9? Make some sentences, putting together words from A, B, and C.**

A If Conway gets better, . . .
   If Conway doesn't get better, . . .

B he will never leave hospital . . .
   he will go back to work . . .

C but another person will build on the graveyard.
   and he will try to build on the graveyard again.
   but he will have bad dreams all his life.
   and the spirits in the graveyard will be happy.
   and he will die as a mad old man.
   but he will be a nicer person.

6 **Do you agree (A) or disagree (D) with these sentences?**

1 Money cannot make you happy.
2 Magic belongs in children's stories, not in the modern world.
3 Life was happier in the old days.
4 It is wrong to put up modern buildings in beautiful, old places.
5 The world changes; people and places must change too.
6 Building in poor countries makes jobs and money for the people who live there.

ABOUT THE AUTHOR

Michael Duckworth is an experienced teacher and writer, who lives and works near Oxford. He has written coursebooks for the Cambridge First Certificate and Proficiency exams, and has also written detective and adventure stories, and ghost stories.

He started writing when he was living in Malaysia. It was there too that he first became interested in old ghost stories and beliefs about magic and spirits, and these ideas are an important part of *Voodoo Island*.

OXFORD BOOKWORMS LIBRARY

Classics • Crime & Mystery • Factfiles • Fantasy & Horror
Human Interest • Playscripts • Thriller & Adventure
True Stories • World Stories

The OXFORD BOOKWORMS LIBRARY provides enjoyable reading in English, with a wide range of classic and modern fiction, non-fiction, and plays. It includes original and adapted texts in seven carefully graded language stages, which take learners from beginner to advanced level. An overview is given on the next pages.

All Stage 1 titles are available as audio recordings, as well as over eighty other titles from Starter to Stage 6. All Starters and many titles at Stages 1 to 4 are specially recommended for younger learners. Every Bookworm is illustrated, and Starters and Factfiles have full-colour illustrations.

The OXFORD BOOKWORMS LIBRARY also offers extensive support. Each book contains an introduction to the story, notes about the author, a glossary, and activities. Additional resources include tests and worksheets, and answers for these and for the activities in the books. There is advice on running a class library, using audio recordings, and the many ways of using Oxford Bookworms in reading programmes. Resource materials are available on the website <www.oup.com/elt/bookworms>.

The *Oxford Bookworms Collection* is a series for advanced learners. It consists of volumes of short stories by well-known authors, both classic and modern. Texts are not abridged or adapted in any way, but carefully selected to be accessible to the advanced student.

You can find details and a full list of titles in the *Oxford Bookworms Library Catalogue* and *Oxford English Language Teaching Catalogues*, and on the website <www.oup.com/elt/bookworms>.

THE OXFORD BOOKWORMS LIBRARY
GRADING AND SAMPLE EXTRACTS

STARTER • 250 HEADWORDS

present simple – present continuous – imperative –
can/cannot, must – going to (future) – simple gerunds …

Her phone is ringing – but where is it?

Sally gets out of bed and looks in her bag. No phone. She looks under the bed. No phone. Then she looks behind the door. There is her phone. Sally picks up her phone and answers it. ***Sally's Phone***

STAGE 1 • 400 HEADWORDS

… past simple – coordination with *and*, *but*, *or* –
subordination with *before*, *after*, *when*, *because*, *so* …

I knew him in Persia. He was a famous builder and I worked with him there. For a time I was his friend, but not for long. When he came to Paris, I came after him – I wanted to watch him. He was a very clever, very dangerous man. ***The Phantom of the Opera***

STAGE 2 • 700 HEADWORDS

… present perfect – *will* (future) – *(don't) have to, must not, could* –
comparison of adjectives – simple *if* clauses – past continuous –
tag questions – *ask/tell* + infinitive …

While I was writing these words in my diary, I decided what to do. I must try to escape. I shall try to get down the wall outside. The window is high above the ground, but I have to try. I shall take some of the gold with me – if I escape, perhaps it will be helpful later. ***Dracula***

... should, may – present perfect continuous – *used to* – past perfect – causative – relative clauses – indirect statements ...

Of course, it was most important that no one should see Colin, Mary, or Dickon entering the secret garden. So Colin gave orders to the gardeners that they must all keep away from that part of the garden in future. ***The Secret Garden***

STAGE 4 • 1400 HEADWORDS

... past perfect continuous – passive (simple forms) – would conditional clauses – indirect questions – relatives with *where/when* – gerunds after prepositions/phrases ...

I was glad. Now Hyde could not show his face to the world again. If he did, every honest man in London would be proud to report him to the police. ***Dr Jekyll and Mr Hyde***

STAGE 5 • 1800 HEADWORDS

... future continuous – future perfect – passive (modals, continuous forms) – *would have* conditional clauses – modals + perfect infinitive ...

If he had spoken Estella's name, I would have hit him. I was so angry with him, and so depressed about my future, that I could not eat the breakfast. Instead I went straight to the old house. ***Great Expectations***

STAGE 6 • 2500 HEADWORDS

... passive (infinitives, gerunds) – advanced modal meanings – clauses of concession, condition

When I stepped up to the piano, I was confident. It was as if I knew that the prodigy side of me really did exist. And when I started to play, I was so caught up in how lovely I looked that I didn't worry how I would sound. ***The Joy Luck Club***

The Pit and the Pendulum and Other Stories

EDGAR ALLAN POE

Retold by John Escott

Everybody has bad dreams, when horrible things move towards you in the dark, things you can hear but not see. Then you wake up, in your own warm bed, and turn over to go back to sleep.

But suppose you wake up on a hard prison floor, in a darkness blacker than the blackest night. You hear the sound of water, you touch a cold metal wall, and smell a wet dead smell. Death is all around you, waiting ...

In these stories by Edgar Allan Poe, death whispers at you from every dark corner, and fear can drive you mad ...

Dead Man's Island

JOHN ESCOTT

Mr Ross lives on an island where no visitors come. He stops people from taking photographs of him. He is young and rich, but he looks sad. And there is one room in his house which is always locked.

Carol Sanders and her mother come to the island to work for Mr Ross. Carol soon decides that there is something very strange about Mr Ross. Where did he get his money from? How can a young man buy an island? So she watches, and she listens – and one night she learns what is behind the locked door.